Christine Pullein-Thompson

Christine and her two sisters
had their first book published
in 1947. To date, Christine
has written 80 best-selling
pony books.

In the past the Pullein-
Thompsons ran two riding
schools, an experience that has
provided a lot of the detail
which makes their stories so
real – Christine feels that it
would be difficult to write a
pony book with no knowledge
of ponies.

Christine Pullein-Thompson
lives in an old parsonage in
Suffolk with her husband,
two ponies and two cats.

British Library Cataloguing in Publication Data

Pullein-Thompson, Christine, *1930-*
    Candy goes to the gymkhana.
    I. Title   II. Rowe, Gavin
    823'.914 [J]
    ISBN 0-7214-1172-X

First edition

Published by Ladybird Books Ltd Loughborough Leicestershire UK
Ladybird Books Inc Auburn Maine 04210 USA
© Text CHRISTINE PULLEIN-THOMPSON MCMLXXXIX
Paperbird is an imprint of Ladybird Books Ltd
© LADYBIRD BOOKS LTD MCMLXXXIX
Printed in England

Candy
goes to the gymkhana

by CHRISTINE PULLEIN-THOMPSON
illustrated by GAVIN ROWE

Paperbird

It was a rainy Saturday morning and too wet for any of the Fraser children to be riding Candy, the family pony.

Instead they had taken over the kitchen of the cheerful, low-beamed cottage where they lived. Liz, the eldest, was browsing through some riding magazines. Neil was making fudge and getting sticky. Vicky, the six year old, was playing with her model farm.

Just as Mum was beginning to complain about the state of her kitchen, Dad added to the confusion by arriving with a large box of groceries. He dumped them on the table and took some papers from his inside pocket.

'Are any of you interested to know that there's a gymkhana in three weeks' time on Handlebury recreation ground?' he asked.

Magazines and fudge-making were instantly forgotten, though Vicky continued playing with her plastic cows and sheep.

'Can we enter?' asked Liz. 'Are there suitable classes?'

'Yes, there's something for everyone. A *Leading Rein* class for Vicky. A *Family Pony* class for Liz. And a *Handy Pony* competition for Neil.'

He handed over the papers, which had the details about entering the gymkhana, and the children spread them out on the table to pore over them.

As well as the events Dad had mentioned there were other events, too, that sounded fun.

'We'll have to find out exactly what you have to do in all these events,' said Liz, 'and then start practising straightaway. We don't want to look silly.'

They telephoned Lisa Mere, owner of the school where they had learned to ride, who advised them about the various events.

She suggested that Vicky should enter the *Leading Rein* class and the *Round the World* and *Egg and Spoon* races. For Neil there was the *Handy Pony* competition, and the *Bending* and *Musical Pole* events for riders under ten years old. For Liz there was the *Family Pony* class, the *Run and Lead* competition and the *Open Musical Poles*.

'That sounds quite enough for Candy,' said Mum when they told her their plans.

During the following weeks the children practised hard for their events.

For the *Leading Rein* class, Vicky learned to sit up straight on Candy, holding the reins loosely, toes up, heels down in the stirrups, while the others led the pony round an imaginary ring. Mum told her to keep smiling. 'And whatever you do,' she said, 'don't put your thumb in your mouth.'

Vicky also learned how to do *Round the World*. It entailed being led to the end of the imaginary ring. There she had to kick her feet out of the stirrups, let go of the reins, twirl round until she faced Candy's tail, then back again. After that, feet back in stirrups, reins back in hands and a race to the finish, as fast as Mum or Dad could run. And they had to hold on tight to Candy all the time, that was the rule.

But Vicky found the *Egg and Spoon* race very difficult. She kept dropping the small potatoes they were using instead of eggs.

'I'll put my thumb on the egg,' she said.

'No you won't!' replied Liz.

'I bet everyone else will.'

'That doesn't matter!' Liz retorted. 'It's cheating. And you are not to cheat!'

Neil had discovered that anything could happen in the *Handy Pony* class. During the round, the rider might have to post a letter, carry water in a cup, jump some small fences, lead his pony across some obstacles... anything! Whoever scored the fastest round was the winner.

Mum made him a postbox out of cardboard, and he practised posting letters from Candy's back. He also tried all the other tests he could think of, but there was no telling exactly what the course would be, for it was supposed to be a secret until the day itself.

Liz desperately wanted everything to go well, but she sometimes worried that Mum and Dad would be disappointed if they didn't win anything. Dad, especially, kept saying, 'You're in with a good chance! Candy really knows her stuff!'

She knew that Neil was expecting to win. He could complete his homemade

course for the *Handy Pony* competition in two minutes flat. But if ever she tried to give advice, he would answer something like, 'Shut up, Bossy Boots!' or, 'I'm better than you, anyway!' He seemed to think he would be riding home covered in rosettes and clutching silver cups.

Liz wasn't so sure!

Candy herself put up with all the practising, even though she already knew what to do.

She could weave in and out between poles for the *Bending* race; she knew that, when the music stopped in *Musical Poles*, she had to gallop to the centre of the ring; in fact, she knew more about gymkhanas than all the Frasers put together! She would have lost count of all the rosettes she'd won, had she known how to count!

But she enjoyed all the extra fuss. Liz groomed her every day until her dapples shone and her mane and tail gleamed like polished silver. Mrs Fraser had bought her a new headcollar – it was blue, and there was a tail bandage to match – while Mr Fraser had bought her a new girth.

On the day before the gymkhana, Candy stood patiently for Liz to bathe her. She seemed to know that it was almost gymkhana time! Granny had brought a bag of old-fashioned Reckitt's Blue to put in the rinsing water, which gave an added whiteness to her coat.

Meanwhile, in the kitchen, Neil and Mum were busy cleaning Candy's saddle and bridle, while Vicky polished the stirrups. When Liz and Granny joined them, Mum took a look at the mess in her kitchen and said, 'Next year we'll have a

proper tack room! There'll be a saddle-horse for the saddle, and proper hooks for the bridle and headcollar. We can do the cleaning in there!'

'And we'll have another pony, so that Neil and I can ride together!' added Liz.

'A black one,' put in Neil, 'that won't show the dirt! And we'll go to lots of Pony Club Rallies...'

'...and become experts!' Liz finished triumphantly.

'Next year...' said Mum, with a smile at Granny.

★   ★   ★

When they rose at six o'clock the next morning there was a fine drizzle falling. Neil picked out Candy's hooves, while Liz fetched a sponge and wiped off the dirt that had mysteriously appeared on her coat during the night.

Then Liz took some grey thread, a needle and pair of scissors to begin the job of plaiting Candy's mane. Mum had told her to make either seven or nine plaits. 'An uneven number, anyway,' she had said.

First Liz dropped the needle, which immediately disappeared into the straw covering the floor of Candy's stable. She had to go indoors to fetch another, and soon managed to prick her finger. It seemed to bleed more than usual, and the blood made a mark on Candy's neck where the hairs were almost white.

'Why don't you help, Neil?' she complained as she sponged Candy's neck clean again. 'Why not thread the needle, at least? I have to do everything! Oh, no!' she suddenly exclaimed. 'Now you've made me drop the scissors!'

At last the job was done. Nine long and rather fat plaits sat on Candy's neck. These, plus the plaited forelock, made an even number. But Liz no longer cared!

In the meantime, Mum had packed a picnic lunch. Dad kept out of everybody's way until nine o'clock, when it was time for Liz and Neil to set off.

Luckily it had stopped raining as Neil fetched the bike, for he and Liz were to hack over to the gymkhana, each riding half the distance while the other cycled. Mum and Dad were to take Vicky in the car.

Liz rode the first half, and after about twenty minutes dismounted for Neil to take over while she cycled. Then at last they could see flags and rows of horse boxes in the distance. Candy pricked her ears and hurried on.

The Handlebury recreation ground was crammed with horse boxes and trailers, from which beautiful horses and ponies were emerging swathed in rugs and bandages, their manes expertly plaited. Competitors were bustling about, and many of them were perfectly turned out in dark coats. A loudspeaker was already giving out orders and urging competitors to assemble in the collecting ring.

'Oh, golly!' said Liz. 'It's much bigger than I expected.'

'You're telling me!' replied Neil.

'Everyone looks *so* rich!'

Mum and Dad had passed them on the way, with Vicky waving merrily from the back seat, and they were waiting for them as they arrived at the ground.

'Dad's got your numbers,' said Mum. 'They're already calling Vicky's *Leading Rein* class, so we'd better be off to the collecting ring.'

At the collecting ring, Liz soon picked out the ponies that were going to win. Their manes were in tiny, tight plaits, all the same size – not at all like Candy's fat little sausages. Their riders wore dark coats, gloves, well fitting jodhpurs and polished boots. Vicky didn't even have a jacket! Their leaders were also turned out in jackets and hats. Mum was wearing shirt, trousers and trainers!

But Vicky didn't notice any of this. She was delighted when she was called first into the centre of the ring, and thought she had already won. 'We're first! Isn't that lovely? Will we get a rosette?' she asked Mum. Mum shook her head and soon other competitors had joined her in a long line. Some of the ponies they rode were as round as barrels; some were old, with grey muzzles; one of the bays needed shoeing; a three year old black pony seemed very thin. Others were happy and loved and in fine condition.

The judge went round and told some of the riders to parade their ponies in a small circle in front of her. These, it seemed, were the likely winners and, although she

sat up straight, smiled, and remembered
not to suck her thumb, Vicky was not
among them.

While the ponies were parading, the
judge – a rather large lady wearing a felt
hat – spoke to the other riders.

'Better luck next year, dear,' she said to
Vicky.

Then the parading ponies formed a long
line in front of the rest, while anxious
friends and parents rushed into the ring to
give them a quick groom and polish before
the final examination. The judge then
began to feel the ponies' legs and open
their mouths to examine their teeth.

Candy tossed her head. She obviously hated being on the back row.

'Never mind, Candy!' said Mum. 'You're still the best!'

'And the prettiest,' Vicky added.

At last the back row of ponies was sent out of the ring. Liz was waiting and moaning, 'Oh, my plaits did look awful! Poor old Candy!'

'I didn't want to win, anyway,' said Vicky, starting to suck her thumb!

There was time to groom Candy once more before Liz entered the ring for the *Family Pony* class. Several of her friends from Lisa Mere's riding school were entering, too, and they did nothing to help Liz's confidence.

'Whoever did your pony's plaits?' cried Alice Greenfield. 'Aren't they a mess!'

'I did them,' replied Liz. 'I've never done them before.'

'Someone should give you a lesson,' sneered Jane Baird. 'They're much too big, among other things.'

'Anyway,' added Alice, 'you don't even need plaits for this class.'

The large lady in the felt hat was judging this class, too. She inspected Candy's tack and gave a sigh. She ran her hand between Candy's front legs and sighed again. 'You've forgotten to groom her here,' she said. 'And there's some grease on the inside of your saddle flaps.'

Liz could have wept.

She then had to give a 'show' to demonstrate the pony's obedience and skill. She tried to copy what the other riders were doing, sliding down over the pony's tail, trotting in a small circle, jumping a small fence.

'Well done!' said the judge after Liz had completed her 'show'. She gave Candy a pat and continued, 'But I'm afraid your pony is too small for this class. A Family Pony should be big enough for all the family to ride!'

Liz felt thoroughly down in the dumps as she rode out of the ring.

'It's hopeless!' she said to Neil. 'We're not going to win anything.'

But Neil had other ideas!

'Give me the hat, Liz,' he said. He and Liz, whose heads were luckily the same size, had to share a hat. 'I'm going to win the *Handy Pony* class!'

Neil looked full of confidence when he began his round, but one of the very first tests involved throwing a potato into a bucket. Neil missed the bucket completely! He had to dismount, retrieve the potato, remount and throw it in all over again. Candy then jumped the fence perfectly, but Neil was unable to post his letter at a gallop, which other competitors could do; nor could he cut the corners as well as they did. So he took exactly one minute to complete the course, whereas the fastest times (chalked up on a board by the entrance to the ring) were thirty five and forty seconds!

Neil was furious when Mum said that he could have only one go. 'But some of the others are having three, Mum,' he complained.

'Think of Candy!' Mum said. 'She has a lot to do today – she's not here just for you! Don't be selfish!'

'I want...' Neil began, but his father interrupted.

'If you don't do as you're told, young man, you'll be going straight home!'

25

Neil was rather sulky as they sat eating their picnic lunch. But he cheered up when Mum and Dad told him he could enter the *Clear Round* jumping competition – if he was willing to pay the entry fee himself.

'I only have to do a clear round to get a rosette!' he said, smiling again.

Unfortunately, Candy went round the course like the wind – much faster than she was able to go in the paddock at home. As a result, Neil lost first his stirrups and then his reins. However, Candy had cleared every fence with ease!

But when Neil asked for his rosette, the judge said, 'Sorry! Your pony did her best but she took the wrong course. After all, she can't be expected to read the numbers on the fences. You're supposed to do that!'

Neil was fuming. It now looked as though he wasn't going to win a rosette, after all. When Granny arrived to join them for the rest of the afternoon, she took one look at his face and said, 'Why are you looking so serious? If at first you

don't succeed, try, try again. Anyway,' she
added, feeding Candy with a carrot she
had brought with her, 'being a nice person
is much more important than winning!'

The next event in which Candy was involved was Vicky's *Round the World* competition.

She did very well in it, but she simply wasn't fast enough. The other competitors were able to swing round in the saddle in one quick twirl. In spite of the rules, they didn't even stop to pick up their reins on the way back, or bother to put their feet into the stirrups.

But Vicky was still smiling when she rode out of the ring.

'Last again!' she called out cheerfully.

Soon she was back in the ring again, this time for the *Egg and Spoon* race. However, she didn't even pretend to be doing it properly, but kept the china egg firmly in place with her thumb all the way round.

She was disqualified.

'Pity she didn't keep her thumb in her mouth!' giggled Liz, who was feeling much happier now that she had given up expecting to win.

★   ★   ★

Neil didn't do well in the *Musical Poles* event either.

This event involved cantering round and round the ring until the music stopped, then galloping into the middle and holding onto a pole. But there was always one pole too few for the riders, so the one who failed to grab a pole was out of the competition.

Unfortunately, when the music stopped and Neil went for the nearest pole, a fat girl on a bay pony got there first and held onto it proudly, smiling triumphantly at Neil as he trotted out of the ring. He had been eliminated.

So he knew now that his last chance of doing well would come in the under-tens *Bending* event. When the competitors were called, he lined Candy up, waiting to spring into action.

Candy, too, seemed to be aware that she had not so far won a single rosette. So on the word GO she raced forward to the line of seven poles, which were stuck into the ground about twenty four feet apart. Then she began weaving in and out between them, going so close to them that Neil almost had one down with his knee. At the last pole she turned quickly and raced back to the start as fast as she could gallop.

Neil was in the finals!

Liz ducked under the ring rope and ran over to him.

'You were marvellous!' she said. 'Did you hear me shouting?'

'Sort of,' said Neil, who hadn't.

'Even if you don't win,' Liz continued, 'at least you've beaten Alice Greenwood and Jane Baird. Horrid things. I used to think they were my friends.'

'It was Candy who beat them,' replied Neil truthfully. 'She just carried me along!'

When they lined up for the finals, Neil crouched forward like a jockey. At that moment he wanted to win more than anything else in the world. He gritted his teeth and pressed his knees hard against the saddle.

Candy went into action so quickly that Neil immediately lost his stirrups. But Candy was in full control and he didn't need them. She turned like an eel round the last of the seven poles and galloped back, ears flat against her head. A black pony was racing neck and neck with her, but Candy's nose was ahead when they reached the winning post.

Even above the noise of the crowd he could hear everyone screaming, 'Well done, Neil!' and 'Hurray!' He jumped down from Candy's back and flung his arms around her neck. She was blowing hard, but her head was up and her eyes were shining.

When his name was called he remounted and rode back into the ring to receive his first-ever rosette. He was also handed a small brown envelope. Meanwhile, over the loudspeaker came the announcement, 'First in the under-tens *Bending* race, Neil Fraser riding Candy.'

How the family cheered as Neil cantered round the ring with the red rosette on Candy's bridle! Dad took a photograph, and Liz had some pony cubes ready as a reward for Candy.

When Neil opened the brown envelope, he discovered that he had won five pounds.

'Look!' he cried, hardly able to believe it.

'Well done, Neil!' said Dad.

'Half of it really belongs to Candy,' Neil admitted, remembering how the pony had galloped her heart out for him.

★ ★ ★

The open events took place next. In her heart, Liz knew she stood no chance of winning anything. Most of the competitors were much older than herself.

All the same, she managed to reach the last ten in the *Musical Poles*, but after she was eliminated she loosened Candy's girths and let the pony graze. The red rosette was still on the bridle and a chubby-faced boy asked her what she had won.

'It's not mine,' Liz answered. 'My brother won it.'

'I didn't win anything, either,' said the boy.

Suddenly Liz felt quite cheerful again, because it reminded her that not everyone can win a prize. There have to be losers if there are to be winners.

'It's been a lovely day, hasn't it?' she remarked before preparing Candy for her last event, the *Run and Lead* race.

When she entered the collecting ring, it was already full of riders. Some were friendly. Others were too snooty to speak, with hats tipped forward and noses in the air.

The butterflies were fluttering in Liz's stomach as the ring steward explained the procedure. There were to be three heats of twelve riders. The first four in each heat would go forward to the final.

Liz was in the first heat, knowing that she was too inexperienced to win and that Candy was too small. Nevertheless, they were well up with the others during the first part of the event, thanks to Candy's galloping speed. But Liz was slow to dismount and was almost last into the final part, in which the competitors ran alongside their ponies to the finishing line. But she quickly started to gain. She found herself running as she had never run before!

The family was cheering her on, but Liz didn't hear them.

Without a glance to left or right, she flew like an arrow with Candy cantering by her side. She passed the chubby-faced boy, a girl with plaits, a boy who looked about fifteen, and a girl in trainers... Then suddenly, it was over.

Panting for breath, she saw that Neil had ducked under the ropes to join her. 'You're through!' he was yelling joyfully. 'You were fourth!'

While the other heats were being run, Neil told her that most of the riders had kicked off their stirrups during the gallop, well before it was time to dismount. Also, that when they had leaped from the ponies' backs they had kept hold of the reins by carrying them over their ponies' heads as they jumped. Liz decided that she would try the same tactics in the final.

Soon she was lining up again. Candy was tiny compared with some of the other ponies, but she was tensed up and ready to race. Then they were off, with twelve sets of hoofs pounding the turf. Liz remembered to kick her feet out of the stirrups in plenty of time, and to leap off taking the reins with her.

She stumbled, but then began to run like the wind.

She could hear the roar of the watching crowd, though she wasn't able to pick out individual voices.

'Faster, faster, faster, faster!' Neil was yelling.

'Liz, Liz, Liz, Liz!' cried Vicky.

'Goodness, that girl can run!' cried Dad.

'And she's so much smaller than the others!' said Mum, who was quite moist-eyed as she watched her daughter race to the finish.

But Liz fell at the line. It was almost as though she had run herself to a standstill, having nothing left to give. She instinctively rolled herself up into a ball as hoofs pounded past her head.

Mr Fraser dashed forward to grab Candy, and Liz was quickly up on her feet again. 'I'm so sorry, so terribly sorry!' she said. 'I don't know why I fell. I must have tripped.'

Dad held Candy's reins in one hand and put an arm round Liz's shoulder. 'You ran a fine race,' he said. 'That's what counts!'

Then the ring steward was by their side. 'Well done!' he said. 'I just want to tell you that you were first. So, please remount for the presentation.'

Liz had fallen over the finishing line and into first place!

She rode proudly into the ring with the three other winners, and the show official said, 'What a wonderful pony!' as he attached the red rosette to Candy's bridle. Then he handed Liz a brown envelope.

Riding round the ring while the spectators applauded was the sort of moment that Liz had dreamed about. She was also proud when Lisa Mere called out, 'Well done, Liz!' as Candy cantered by.

Afterwards she gave the brown envelope to her father. 'I expect it's another five pounds,' she said. 'You paid the entry fees, Dad, so it really belongs to you.'

'No!' replied her father. 'You won it. It's yours. Use it to buy something you need.'

★   ★   ★

The last event of the day was the consolation race. Vicky rode Candy, who was now very tired, and Mum ran alongside. They came in fifth, but every rider in the event was given a pink rosette. Vicky was thrilled.

'I knew I'd win!' she said.

On the way home, Neil started making plans for the next year.

'We'll do much better,' he said. 'I'm definitely going to win the *Handy Pony* class as well as the *Bending* and *Musical Poles*.'

Liz didn't reply for a moment. Then she said, 'We mustn't become horrible, though. I would hate us to be like some of them there today. They only cared about winning. They didn't care about their ponies. They just rode them up and down all day, jerking at their poor mouths and kicking them with their heels.'

'They had lots of money,' said Neil. 'If that's what money does, it's not worth it.'

When they arrived home, Mum was already making a special mash for Candy, full of grated apple and sliced carrots. Liz and Neil took off the tired pony's tack and gave her a drink. They brushed off the saddle marks and watched her roll over and over in the dew-damp grass.

Later, they all went out to give Candy her feed.

Liz was thinking that the sound of the pony contentedly munching her feed was the loveliest sound in the world.

Neil was thinking about his victories at the next gymkhana.

Vicky was thinking that her pink rosette was much prettier than the red ones.

But at last it was time to go in.

Candy had been to the gymkhana and given every one of them a wonderful day!

If you have enjoyed this story, read:
CANDY STOPS A TRAIN
by Christine Pullein-Thompson

When Liz, Neil and Vicky Fraser
discover that the family pony,
Candy, is missing from her
paddock, little do they know what
a frantic race against time lies in
store for them...

Other PAPERBIRD titles:

Never a witch's cat
by ANN TURNBULL

A group of cats, compelled by the call of the moon one Hallowe'en, venture out, only to be caught by The Witch. They are destined to become witches' cats unless they can break free from her power...

Stone of mystery
by BETTE MEYRICK

Yvonne is given a pendant of stone mined from the same Welsh hillside that provided the stone for Stonehenge. But it seems that someone from the past desperately wants the pendant returned...

Phantom from the past
by SUSAN PRICE

When the school decides to have a Victorian day as part of their history lesson, all the children and teachers dress in Victorian costume to re-enact a school day in the nineteenth century. But as the day wears on, one of the teachers seems to be taking things too seriously...

Night school
by ROBERT SWINDELLS

Why are things often moved or missing from the classroom? Why do the cleaners clean the school twice? Lucy and Jen decide to return to school one evening to find out who or WHAT uses their school at night...